MW00910854

ONE-MINUTE PUZZLES TO FUZZLE YOUR BRAIN

THE MESMERIZING MAZE CHALLENGE

BY ROBIN PREISS GLASSER

Lowell House
Juvenile
Los Angeles

CONTEMPORARY BOOKS
Chicago

For my mother, with love, who has always guided me down the better path.

Copyright © 1995 by RGA Publishing Group, Inc. Illustrations copyright © 1995 by Robin Preiss Glasser. All rights reserved. No part of this work may be reproduced or transmitted in any form or by any means, electronic or mechanical, including photocopying and recording, or by any information storage or retrieval system, except as may be expressly permitted by the 1976 Copyright Act or in writing by the publisher.

Requests for such permissions should be addressed to:
Lowell House Juvenile
2029 Century Park East, Suite 3290
Los Angeles, CA 90067

Lowell House books can be purchased at special discounts when ordered in bulk for premiums or special sales. Contact Department VH at the above address.

Manufactured in the United States of America

ISBN: 1-56565-254-1

10 9 8 7 6 5 4 3 2 1

INTRODUCTION

Take the *One-Minute Puzzle* challenge
and try to go from start to finish in no
more than a minute! You'll have *hours*
of fun following the twists and turns
of these mesmerizing mazes, but you
only have a minute to solve each one.
Hurry—your time is running out!

PLEASE RETURN TO
BRUCE ~~son~~

1

If you dare, enter this haunted house, but take no more than a minute to go from start to finish. Beware of loose bricks, rickety boards, and ghosts along the way!

START FINISH

2

The fire-breathing dragon is fast approaching
the poor princess, who is trapped in his lair.
In a minute or less, show the princess the way
out of the gate—before it's too late!

3

It should take the cat burglar no more than a minute to climb the castle wall. Once there, he will join the terrace ball and mingle with the unsuspecting guests!

4

It will take one minute for this
gruesome spider to crawl over
to devour its prey. Help the
beautiful butterfly to escape
from the sticky web.

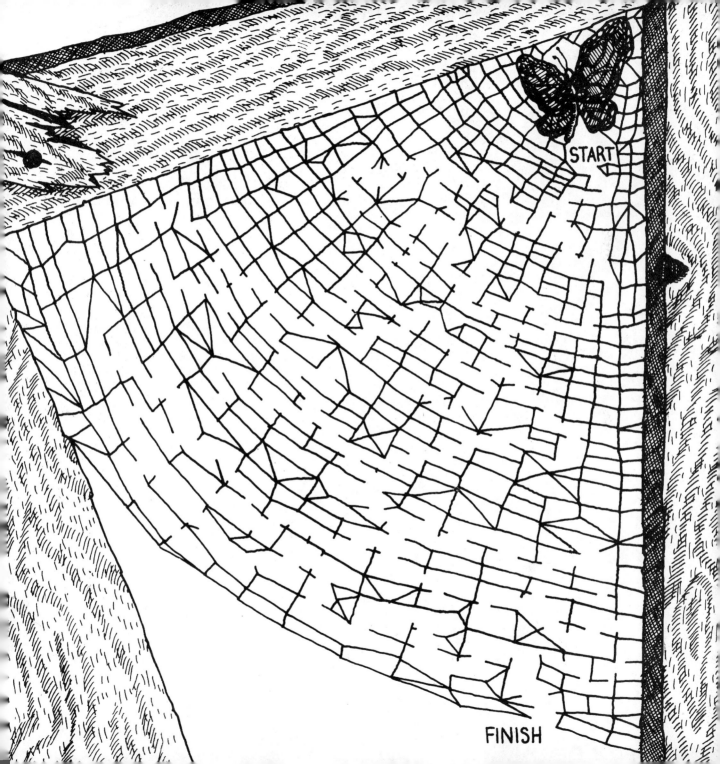

START

FINISH

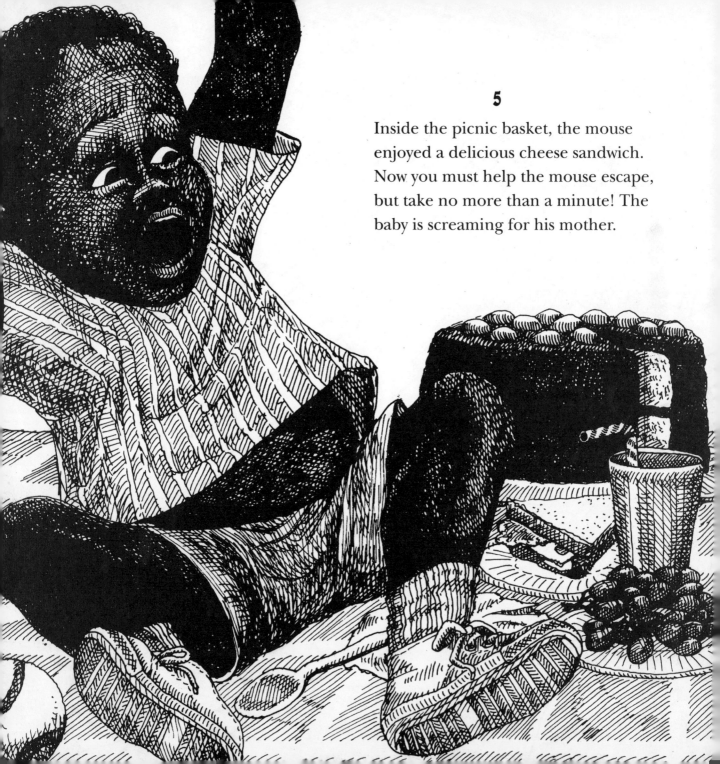

5

Inside the picnic basket, the mouse
enjoyed a delicious cheese sandwich.
Now you must help the mouse escape,
but take no more than a minute! The
baby is screaming for his mother.

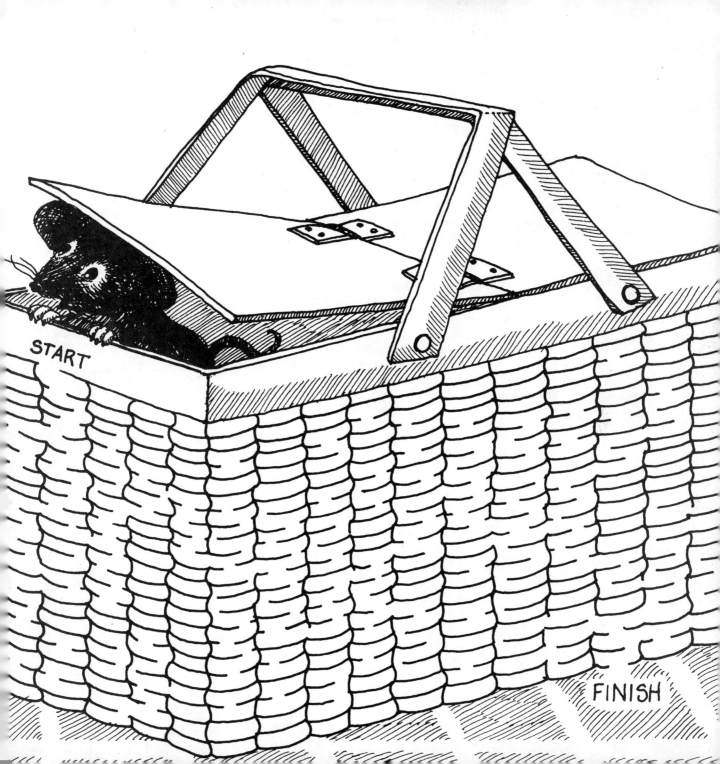

START

FINISH

START

FINISH

6

In a minute or less, help these children find their way to freedom through the mesmerizing twists and turns of the garden labyrinth. Darkness is fast approaching, and there are lots of obstacles along the way!

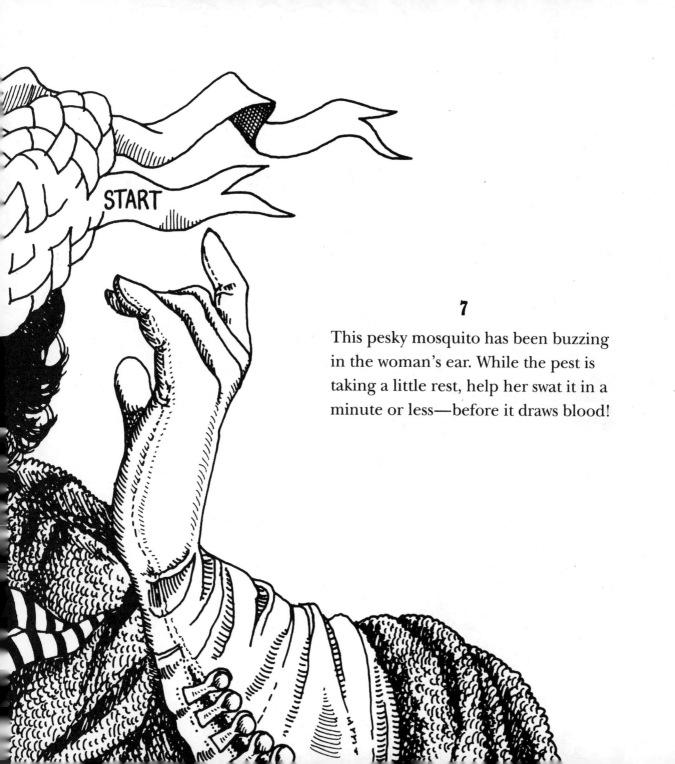

START

7

This pesky mosquito has been buzzing in the woman's ear. While the pest is taking a little rest, help her swat it in a minute or less—before it draws blood!

8

Poor Princess Morning Dove has gone and lost her evening glove. Help her find it in no more than a minute—before she's late for a date with the prince!

9

Help the children find their way to safety in a minute or less. But beware of the dangers at every turn—venomous snakes, prickly cactuses, and ferocious dinosaurs.

START

FINISH

10

An itchy foot is about to awaken this girl from a deep, dreamy sleep. In no more than a minute, find your way across the bedclothes and help the drowsy child reach her toes.

In a minute, this egg-devouring snake will have slithered down the tree to the bird's nest. Help the crow get to her children in time—before the snake has them for dinner!

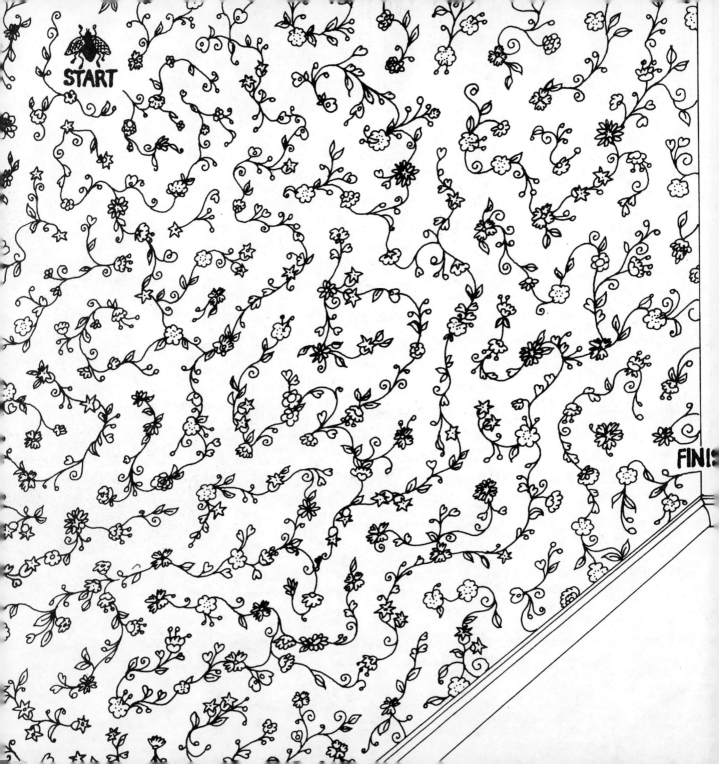

12

The flowered wallpaper has confused the
forlorn fly. In no more than a minute,
help the fly find a way to the open window,
before it's closed by the upstairs maid.

FINISH

START

13

The perplexed prince's ladder is too short! You must help him scale the tower wall to rescue the fair maiden. But take a minute or less, because the maiden's cruel captor is climbing the tower stairs!

FINISH

14

The hasty horsefly has bitten the zebra. It must escape before the angry zebra kills it with a swat of her tail. Take no more than a minute to show the horsefly the way to freedom.

START

It's a race to see who can climb to the top of the pyramid in a minute or less—you or the nomads. Can you get there first?

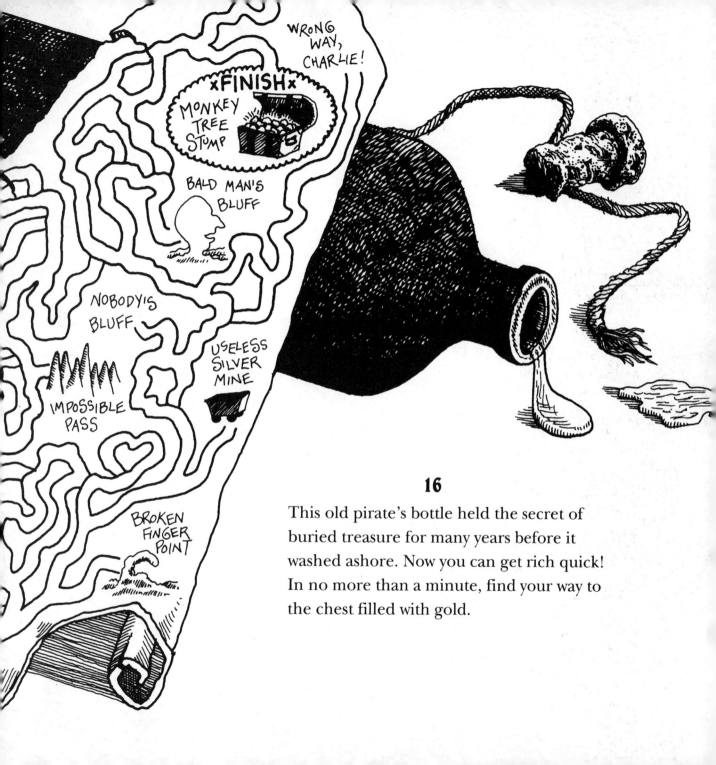

16

This old pirate's bottle held the secret of buried treasure for many years before it washed ashore. Now you can get rich quick! In no more than a minute, find your way to the chest filled with gold.

17

On this hot summer day, the dairy farmer has no time to take a wrong turn while bringing his milk products to town. Show him the way from the farm to the warehouse in the city—but take no more than a minute!

START

FINISH

START

18

The captain of the tall ship needs your help to navigate around the volcanic islands. Take a minute or less to show him the way to port—the large volcano is starting to erupt!

FINISH

19

Can you come to the rescue? It will be
dark soon, and the little girl's curious
cat climbed up too high in the tall,
knotty tree. Help the poor kitty get
down in less than a minute.

START

FINISH

START

20

There's a rockslide! You have one minute
to help this fleeing couple find their way
to town. Watch out for steep paths, falling
rocks, and wild animals along the way!

NISH

FINISH?

FINISH?

21

The befuddled boy can't remember where he left his brand-new bicycle. So he won't be in trouble when he gets home, take no more than a minute to help him find the correct path to his bike.

START

ANSWERS

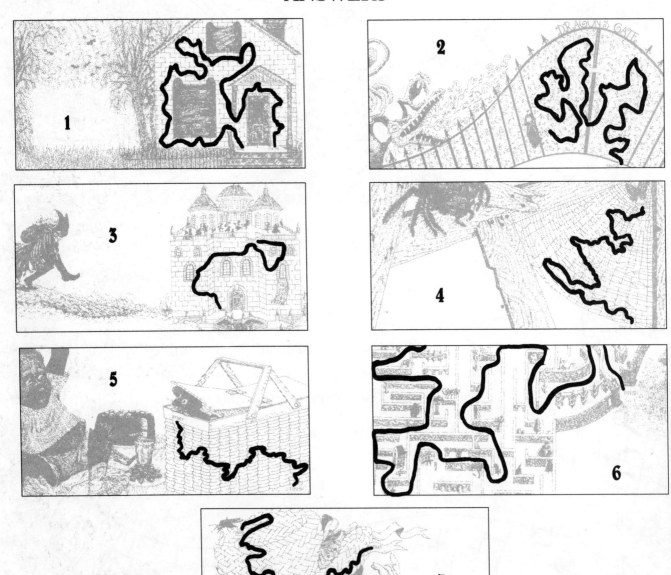

ANSWERS

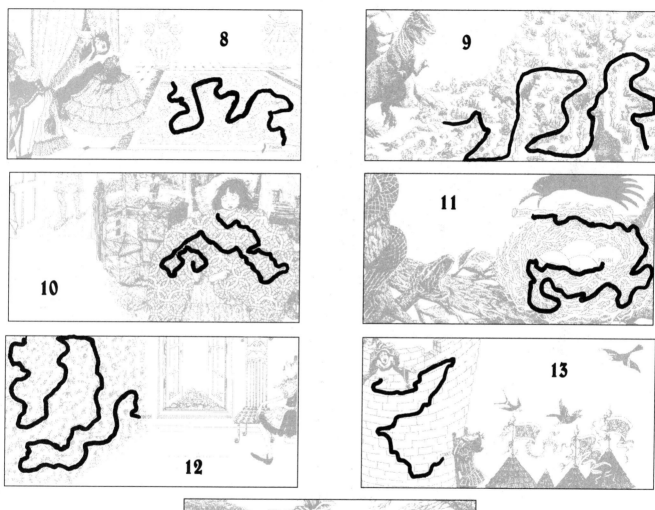

ANSWERS

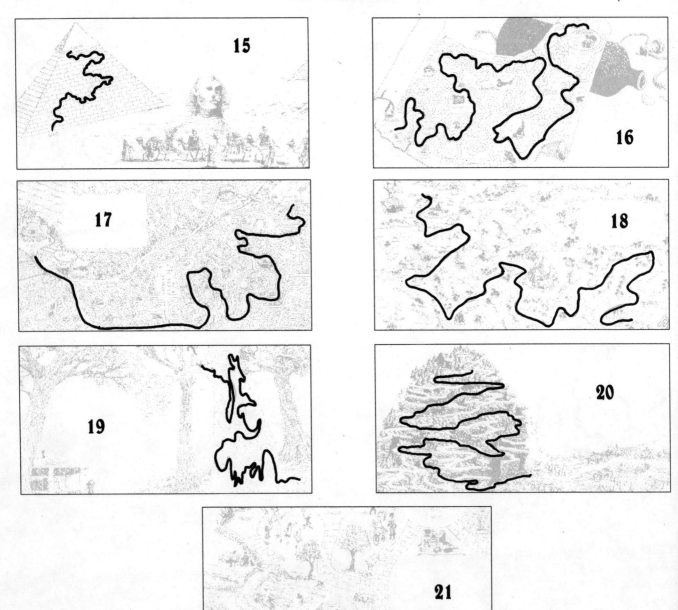